This Little Tiger book belongs to:

_____

_____

_____

For my godsons, Jacob and Noah,
who I love more than Christmas
- E H

To Boaz and the
marvellous Mesegs x
- T W

LITTLE TIGER PRESS LTD,
an imprint of the Little Tiger Group
1 Coda Studios, 189 Munster Road, London SW6 6AW
Imported into the EEA by Penguin Random House Ireland,
Morrison Chambers, 32 Nassau Street, Dublin D02 YH68
www.littletiger.co.uk

First published in Great Britain 2020
This edition published 2021

Text by Ellie Hattie • Text copyright © Little Tiger Press Ltd 2020
Illustrations copyright © Tim Warnes 2020 • Visit Tim Warnes at www.timwarnes.com
Tim Warnes has asserted his right to be identified as the illustrator
of this work under the Copyright, Designs and Patents Act, 1988
A CIP catalogue record for this book is available from the British Library

Printed in China • LTP/1800/4771/0322
4 6 8 10 9 7 5

I Love You more than Christmas

ELLIE HATTIE • TIM WARNES

Santa, stop here!

LITTLE TIGER

LONDON

There was a chill in the air and frost on the trees.
Something special was on its way!

"IT'S NEARLY CHRISTMAS!"
whooped Little Bear. "And I LOVE it!"

"I love wrapping, and ribbons, and balls of bright string,
And gift tags, and glitter – the joy that they bring!
I love giving presents, and getting them too,
But the thing that I love more than Christmas is—"

"It's Mrs Postbear," cried Mummy Bear.
"What will be in her sack today?"

"CHRISTMAS CARDS!"

cheered Little Bear.

"There's one here from Granny, and Great Aunty Sue,
I love cards and packages, oh yes I do!
But the thing that I love more than Christmas is—"

"I'm home!"
cried Daddy Bear, stomping through the door.

"That's the biggest, bushiest, **greenest** tree I've ever seen!" gasped Little Bear.

So while they wrestled it into the front room . . .

. . . Mummy scrambled up into the attic to find
the decorations, singing as she went.

"I love baubles, and tinsel,
and lights on a string,
Candy canes, stockings,
and all of the things,

That make Christmas perfect,
oh yes I do!
But the thing that I love more
than Christmas is–"

"Goodness me!"
Mummy Bear cried
when she saw the size
of the tree.

It really was
a whopper!

But many paws make light work,
and in no time at all the tree
looked spectacular.

"Well, fluff my fur!" sighed Daddy Bear contentedly.
"*What an exceedingly talented family we are.
There's just one thing missing . . .*"

"*A bright shiny
star!*"
sang Mummy Bear,
when . . .

BEEP-BEEP!

BEEP-BEEP!

went the oven.

"By my ears!"
gasped Mummy Bear.
"It's time to ice the
Christmas cake!
All paws to the kitchen!"

In a flurry of sprinkles and
icing sugar, Daddy Bear exclaimed,
"I love Christmas pudding, and mince pies and sherry!
They fill up my tummy and make me feel merry.
I love Christmas goodies – yes really, it's true –
but the thing that I love more than Christmas is—"

Tra-la-la.

"The carol singers are here!"
giggled Little Bear, flinging the door open wide
to let the sweet music bounce down the hall.

"We love singing carols,
they make us feel jolly.
We love bright red berries,
and pine cones, and holly . . .

We bring festive spirit
to all that we do.
But the thing that we love
more than Christmas is—"

"Cookies and
hot chocolate, anybody?"
Mummy Bear called, rushing
out from the kitchen.

"Yes please!" cheered the carol singers,
and they skipped merrily inside.

Well, the bears and
their visitors had such a ball,
But suddenly somebody
called from the hall,

"Isn't it dark?
And it's started to snow,
So I think that it's time
that we all ought to go."

Daddy Bear had just
shut the door when BONG!
the clock struck bedtime.

So Mummy Bear lifted
Little Bear onto her back and
they trooped up the stairs . . .

. . . where they all got ready for bed.

"Mummy and Daddy," yawned Little Bear,
"I LOVE, LOVE, LOVE Christmas!
All the happiness, laughter, friends old and new.
The sleigh bells, and reindeer, and Santa Claus too.
But the thing that I love more than Christmas is—"

"YOU!"

laughed Mummy and Daddy Bear,
giving Little Bear a great big hug.

Because, as everybody knows,
the gift of Christmas is only as wonderful
as the love that it's wrapped in.

Merry Christmas, everyone!